A Penny For Barnaby

by Wendy W. Rouillard

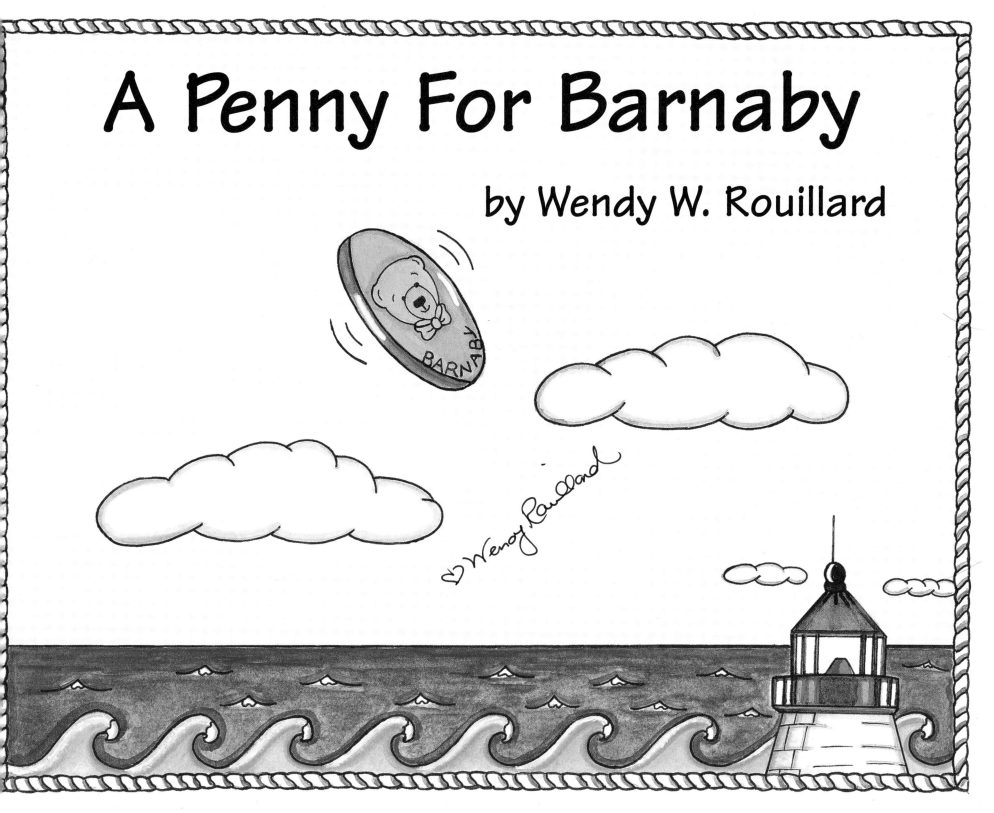

For ordering information, write or telephone:

BARNABY & COMPANY PUBLISHING AND PRODUCTIONS, L.L.C.

P.O. Box 3198
Nantucket, MA 02584
Tel: 508-228-5114
Email: barnaby@nantucket.net

ISBN 0-9642836-7-0
Library of Congress Catalog Card Number: 98-92485

Summary: Stranded on an unknown island, Barnaby's lucky penny mysteriously brings him and his friends safely home to Nantucket.

Note: A PENNY FOR BARNABY is based on the Nantucket tradition of throwing a penny overboard when leaving the Island in order to insure a safe return. Others, to my knowledge, who have previously written about this subject are: Brinton Turkle, Jane Tompkins, and Loren Brock.

Special thanks to my husband, Illya, for his patience, guidance and constant enthusiasm; to my Mother for her continuous help and support; and to Cecil Sanford for all of her time, help, and advice.

BARNABY BOOK #3
Second Edition

Visit Barnaby's Web Site!
www.barnabybear.com

~For my Father

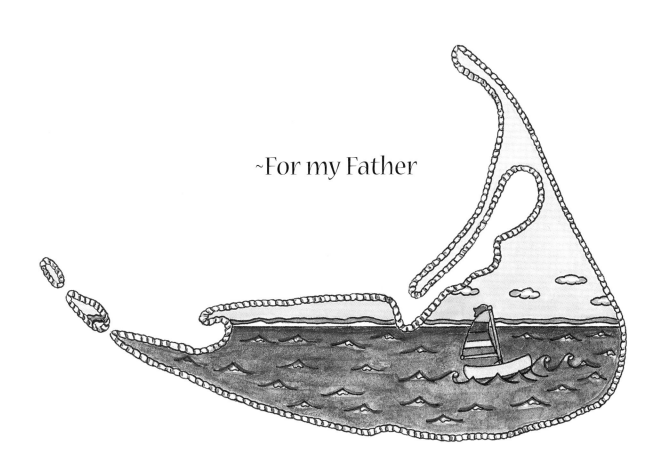

There is not much to do on a stormy summer day on Nantucket Island, and Barnaby was about as bored as a bear could be.

"Maybe I should take a walk," thought Barnaby.

As Barnaby strolled down the wet street, heavy rain was falling from the dark clouds, and the wind was so strong that he could barely hold onto his umbrella.

When Barnaby came to the corner of Main Street, he saw something shining on the ground. As he looked more closely, he saw that it was an amazingly shiny penny.

Barnaby bent down to pick up the penny…

...and as he held it in his hand the weather instantly changed. The rain stopped, and the storm clouds turned to bright blue sky. The birds started chirping, and the flowers sprang into full bloom. It was now the perfect summer day on Nantucket Island.

Barnaby looked down at the penny he was holding in his hand and thought, "Wow! I have found a very lucky penny!"

Barnaby put the penny in his pocket, and as he continued his walk down Main Street, he met his friends, Baisley the Bear, Baxter the Basset Hound, and Cecile the Seagull standing outside the newspaper store.

"What a beautiful day it turned out to be," said Barnaby with a smile. "Why don't we all go for an afternoon sail?"

So the four friends went their separate ways to spend the morning gathering everything they needed for their afternoon sail. They were to meet at noon down on Old North Wharf.

When Baisley, Baxter, and Cecile arrived at the Wharf, Barnaby was there waiting for them.

"Do we have everything we need?" asked Barnaby.

"I sure do hope so," said Baisley.

"What did you bring, Barnaby?" asked Baxter.

"I brought a penny," said Barnaby. "It's not just an ordinary penny. It is a lucky penny."

"What are we going to do with a lucky penny?" asked Cecile.

"Sailors had a tradition in the old days," said Barnaby. "Before they went on a long voyage, they threw coins into the ocean hoping to make the powerful gods of the sea happy. The gods would then allow them to return home safely. So, as we sail around Brant Point Lighthouse, I will toss my lucky penny overboard. My lucky penny will bring us safely back to Nantucket."

But no one believed Barnaby's story. They didn't even believe he really had a lucky penny. To them it just looked like any other penny.

Barnaby, Baisley, Baxter, and Cecile hopped onboard the boat and sailed swiftly out of the harbor.

Barnaby, the Captain, took his usual place at the bow of the boat.

Baxter, who is always hungry, began to nibble on a ham and cheese sandwich.

Cecile took hold of the tiller and kept an eye on the fishing pole off the stern of the boat.

And Baisley began to play her guitar, singing: "We sail, we sail, we sail the deep blue sea."

As the sailboat rounded Brant Point Lighthouse, Barnaby quickly reached into his pocket, took out the shiny penny, and tossed it into the sea.

All of a sudden, Cecile saw that something was tugging on the fishing pole.

"Hey, I think we've caught a fish!" yelled Cecile.

"Hold on tight to the fishing pole," cried Barnaby.

Cecile tried to reel in the fish, but it was too big and too strong.

"I can't hold onto the fishing pole much longer," cried Cecile.

The fish began to pull the sailboat faster and faster out to sea. Barnaby hurried to the stern of the boat to help Cecile hold onto the fishing pole. Baisley and Baxter quickly rushed to help.

All at once, they were pulled out of the sailboat and flung into the air.

"OH NO!" cried Barnaby and Baisley.

"YAHOO!" shouted Baxter.

"YIKES!" groaned Cecile.

The four friends landed in the water with a giant splash. They saw the fog slowly rolling in, and their sailboat quickly drifting away.

"Now what are we going to do?" asked Baisley.

But before anyone could answer, a huge wave swept them up and carried them safely ashore.

Suddenly, the four friends found themselves on the beach. They looked around, but it was so foggy that they did not recognize where they were.

"So much for your lucky penny, Barnaby," said Cecile. "It surely didn't bring us safely back home."

So then Barnaby, Baisley, Baxter, and Cecile poked their heads over the nearest sand dune.

"Where are we?" asked Barnaby.

"I'm scared!" said Baisley.

"There could be wild monsters!" cried Cecile.

"This is so exciting!" said Baxter. "Let's go exploring!"

Baisley and Cecile explored the island, gathering berries and collecting driftwood for a fire.

Barnaby made a fishing pole out of an old piece of rope and a stick which he found on the beach. He began to fish…

…while Baxter tried to catch a crab for dinner.

Eventually, the four of them began having so much fun that they forgot they were stranded.

That evening, they all sat around the open fire cooking the fish which Barnaby had caught, and eating the berries that Baisley and Cecile had picked.

When it grew dark, they sang to the stars and danced in the foggy moonlight.

And then, tired from their busy day, they snuggled together on the beach, and fell asleep to the sound of the breaking waves.

When they awoke in the morning, Barnaby, Baisley, Baxter, and Cecile started to worry about not being able to get home. The fog had not lifted, so no one from Nantucket would be able to look for them.

Barnaby sat down by the sea and gazed out into the thick gray fog. His eyes filled with tears. He wanted to go home.

As the waves splashed against his feet, Barnaby looked down, and there was a penny, shining in the sand. It was his lucky penny! It had washed ashore.

Barnaby leaned over to pick up the penny, and as he held it in his hand, he said aloud:

> I gave this penny to the sea,
> And now it has returned to me,
> Please take me back to the Isle I know,
> A place my heart will never let go.

As Barnaby spoke those words, once again the weather instantly changed. The gray fog lifted, and the warm golden sun began to shine. And there, in front of him, was his sailboat ready to take them home. Barnaby could see Nantucket Harbor in the distance. They had not been far from home after all.

Since that day, Baisley, Baxter, and Cecile truly believe that Barnaby's penny is very lucky.

And, every time they leave the Island of Nantucket and pass by Brant Point Lighthouse, they think of Barnaby's lucky penny which brought them safely back to Nantucket. And as they toss their pennies into the sea, they shout:

"A PENNY FOR BARNABY!"